I SPY ISLAND

Meet Sue and Paul:

Sue Hendra and **Paul Linnet** have been making books together
since 2009 when they came up with *Barry the Fish with Fingers*,
and since then they haven't stopped. If you've ever wondered
which one does the writing and which does the illustrating,
wonder no more . . . they both do both!

For Helen, our editor, a never-ending source of professionalism,
kindness, patience and fun.

SIMON & SCHUSTER

First published in Great Britain in 2021 by Simon & Schuster UK Ltd • 1st Floor, 222 Gray's Inn Road, London, WC1X 8HB
Text and illustrations copyright © 2021 Sue Hendra and Paul Linnet
The right of Sue Hendra and Paul Linnet to be identified as the authors and illustrators of this work
has been asserted by them in accordance with the Copyright, Designs and Patents Act, 1988
A CIP catalogue record for this book is available from the British Library upon request
978-1-4711-9627-0 (PB) • 978-1-4711-9629-4 (eBook) • Printed in China • 10 9 8 7 6 5 4 3 2

I SPY ISLAND

SUE HENDRA & PAUL LINNET

SIMON & SCHUSTER

London New York Sydney Toronto New Delhi

In the middle of the ocean,

miles from anywhere,

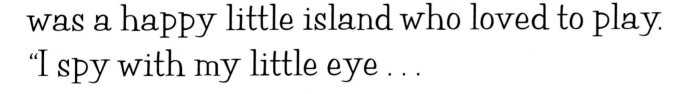

was a happy little island who loved to play.
"I spy with my little eye . . .

something beginning with 'S' . . ."

"Is it a sausage?" asked Glove.
"It's not a shark, is it?"
panicked Bottle.
"I wish it WAS a sausage,"
said Banana.

"It's the sea again, isn't it?" said Bird.
"It might be," said the Island, with a giggle.

"My turn," said Banana. "I spy with my little eye . . .

. . . a funny thing on your chin!"

"Oooh," said the Island, "it must have just washed up. I wonder what it is?"

Everyone gathered around for a closer look.

"It's got legs coming out of its head!" shrieked Bottle.

"I think it's just upside-down," said Bird.

"Can I eat it?" asked Banana.

"I know what it is!" cried Glove.
"I've seen one before.
It's a trouser press . . .
A toucan's vest . . .
A funny nest . . .
A . . . ."

"I'M A TREASURE CHEST!" shouted the box, flipping onto its feet, "and I'm **very** important!

Everyone wants to own me because my treasure is priceless!"

"Errrr, what's treasure?" asked the Island.

"What's treasure?! What's treasure?!"
spat Treasure Chest, throwing open its mouth . . .

BLING!

Everyone was very impressed.

"We haven't a moment to lose," said Treasure Chest. "I'm far too important to stay here. I've got places to be!

Come on, everyone, get to work!

I want flags made out of seaweed....

and signs made out of driftwood."

HELP!

OVER HERE!

JELLY!

As they worked, Treasure Chest
sat alone, guarding its precious treasure.

Finally, they were finished.

"What's next?" said the Island.

"I'm so important that someone will come
looking for me," replied Treasure Chest. "So we wait."
"For how long?" asked the Island.
Treasure Chest thought . . . "For as long as it takes . . ."

Hours passed,

then days.

Eventually, Treasure Chest spoke. "Maybe they're not coming back for me after all," it said, sadly.

We must do something to cheer Treasure Chest up, thought the Island. "Umm . . . how about a game while we wait?"

"A game? Treasure Chests don't play games."

"Oh, go on," said Bird. "We'll throw the ball and you catch it."
"Why?" asked Treasure Chest.

"You'll see," said Banana.

And after a bit of encouragement, Treasure Chest got the hang of it. And then couldn't stop. Next it was races . . .

. . . then hide-and-seek,

and by the end of the day, everyone was exhausted. "I don't think I've ever had this much fun," said Treasure Chest.

And that was just the beginning.
All summer, they built giant
sandcastle kingdoms,

they danced in the moonlight,

they jumped into the sea,

and they laughed;
they laughed A LOT.

"Maybe this isn't such a bad place to be,"
said Treasure Chest. "It's always fun,
blue skies and sunshine . . ."

"I wouldn't be so sure about that," said the Island. "There's a storm coming and I think it's going to be a **big** one . . ."

The sky was getting darker and the wind was starting to blow.

"Everyone hang on to something!" said the Island.

"HELP!" yelled the friends, struggling to hold on.

Soon, the storm was raging
and it raged for days.
Thunder crashed, lightning flashed
and the wind howled.

It was loud and it was scary.

When it was all over and the Island finally
opened its eyes, everything was calm
and quiet . . . too quiet.

"Treasure Chest, where has everyone gone?!"

"We're in here!"
they shouted,
throwing open
Treasure Chest's lid.

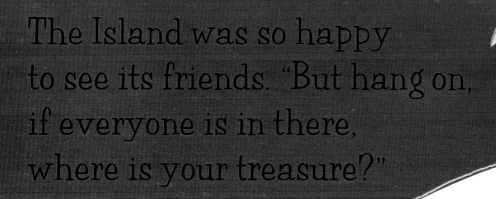

The Island was so happy
to see its friends. "But hang on,
if everyone is in there,
where is your treasure?"

"Well," said Treasure Chest,
"there wasn't room for both."

"But your treasure is priceless!"
said the Island.

"No," smiled Treasure Chest. "I've learnt that
friendship is priceless . . .

. . . and besides, I hid it in your sand!

Let's dig it up and play with it,"
said Treasure Chest.
So they did!

Bird dressed up in it,

Glove got lost in it

and Bottle juggled with it.

"Can I . . . ?"

"NO, Banana, you can't eat it!" everyone said together.

So there they were, in the middle of the ocean, miles from anywhere – a happy little island playing with its friends.

"I spy with my little eye," said the Island, "something beginning with 'S' . . ."

"It better not be the sea again," said Bird.
The Island giggled . . .

"Hang on!" said Treasure Chest.
"What's that I spy on your chin?"

Had something new washed up?

Everyone gathered around for a closer look . . .